Based on the teleplay "Bouncy Tires" by Kevin Del Aguila

Illustrated by Ben Burch

A GOLDEN BOOK • NEW YORK

T#: 429653
randomhousekids.com
ISBN 978-0-553-53891-5
Printed in the United States of America
10 9 8 7 6

One morning at the Axle City Garage, Blaze and AJ were helping their friend Gabby unload a shipment of tires.

"They're silly tires!" Gabby explained
with a giggle.

Inside the crates were dancing tires . . . stinky tires . . . and even feathery chicken tires!

"*Bok-bok-bok!*" clucked the tires as they rolled away.

Blaze and AJ saw Zeg trying to drive down the street. He was having a hard time because his tires had big holes in them!

Blaze pulled out his towing hook. "Hang on," he said. "I'll give you a tow!"

Suddenly, a crate wiggled and jiggled and then burst open! *Boing! Boing!* Four bright green silly tires bounced out.

"Funny tires go up and down," the dinosaur truck laughed. "Zeg like! Zeg want those tires!"

Zeg put on the tires—and started bouncing!
"Blaze? AJ? We have a problem," said
Gabby. "Those tires are the silliest tires of all!
They're super-bouncy tires. Once they start
bouncing, they don't stop!"

"Okay, tires," said Zeg. "No more bouncing!"

But the tires didn't stop. Zeg bounced out of the garage—and straight into traffic!

"Don't worry, Gabby," said Blaze. "We'll find a way to stop those bouncy tires."

"If we're gonna catch Zeg," said AJ, "we need to use Blazing Speed!" Blaze revved his engine, popped his boosters, and—*VROOM!*—took off to save his friend!

"I know how we can save Zeg," said Blaze. "Let's make those bouncy tires stick to the road. We'll use adhesion! Adhesion is when two things stick together."

Blaze unrolled a piece of tape and stuck it right in Zeg's path.

Zeg landed on the tape, but he bounced off
again! The tape was sticky, but not sticky enough.
"Next time we try adhesion, we need something
even stickier," AJ said.
Zeg kept bouncing straight toward a building.
"Uh-oh!" said Blaze. "That's the egg warehouse!"

Zeg crashed through the warehouse, knocking over crates and baskets. "Sorry! Coming through!" he yelled.

The bouncy tires hit a red button. A crane
turned and picked up a huge egg.
"Oh, no!" cried a worker truck. "He just
turned on the Giant Egg Dropper!"

The crane was going to drop the egg, so Blaze raced as fast as he could to save it. He ducked under conveyor belts and weaved past fallen crates and baskets.

When the egg dropped, Blaze reached out
and caught it just in time!

Blaze had saved the giant egg, but he still had to save Zeg.

"We can use adhesion again to stop those tires. Maybe this is sticky enough to work." AJ grabbed a bottle and squeezed out a puddle of glue.

Zeg landed in the glue. The goo splattered all over the tires and slowed Zeg down. But then he sprang up . . . and up . . . and up . . . until— *SNAP!*—he broke free! Just like the tape, the glue couldn't stop his bouncing!

"We're gonna need something even stickier," said AJ.

"Oh, no!" groaned Zeg. The super-bouncy tires were taking him straight toward a bakery—and a beautiful frosted cake!

"Somebody stop him!" cried the baker.

"I've got an idea," said Blaze. "What if we use quick-dry cement? That's the super-stickiest thing I can think of!"

Blaze put together a spiral mixing blade, a rotating drum, and a discharge chute, transforming himself into a cement mixer.

"The sticky cement is mixed and ready to pour!" called AJ.

Blaze tipped the discharge chute. Cement flowed out in a goopy gray puddle.

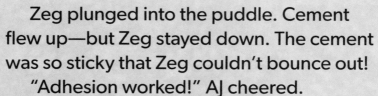

Zeg plunged into the puddle. Cement
flew up—but Zeg stayed down. The cement
was so sticky that Zeg couldn't bounce out!
"Adhesion worked!" AJ cheered.
"Zeg thank Blaze and AJ!" the dinosaur
truck said with a smile.

"You're welcome, big fella!" said Blaze. "Now, what do you say we get you a different set of tires?"

The dinosaur truck nodded. "Zeg like that idea! Zeg like!"

Back at the garage, Gabby replaced the bouncy tires with regular tires. "How do they feel?" she asked.

"*Wheeee!*" Zeg shouted as he cruised around the garage. "No bouncing!"

Blaze and AJ laughed, glad their friend was safely back on the ground!